PLANTS VS. ZOMBIES™

Brain Food

By Brandon T. Snider

HARPER FESTIVAL

An Imprint of HarperCollinsPublishers

www.harpercollinschildrens.com

ISBN 978-0-06-229492-0

Book design by Victor Joseph Ochoa

13 14 15 16 17 LP/RRDH 10 9 8 7 6 5 4 3 2 1

First Edition

Answer key for all activities in this book

can be found on pages 215 to 224.

Hey, everybody! Crazy Dave here! This activity book is crawling with zombies so keep your eyes peeled. But it's got a lot of awesome plants, too! Don't peel those, though, okay? Now get in there and get to business. I'll see you later. I got a thing I gotta do.

Crazy Dave looks a little pale. You should give him some color.

Totally Awesome Trivia

How much do you know about plants? Take a look at the question and see if you can pick the correct answer from the choices below.

Plants get their energy from what?

Sunlight

Electricity

Pollen

Magic

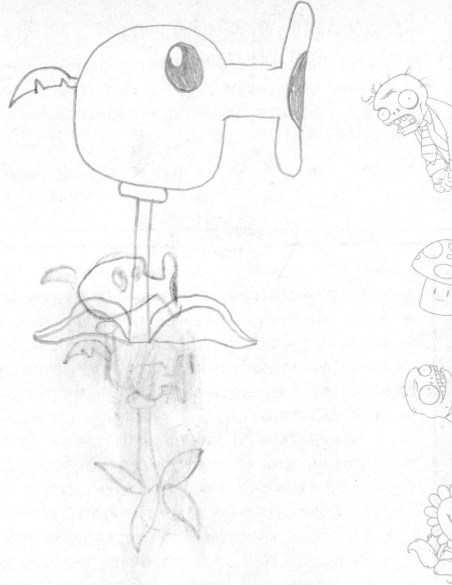

What's your favorite plant or flower? Draw it in the space above!

Secret Message

Cross out the name **PEASHOOTER** every time you see it in the box below. When you spot a letter that doesn't belong, write it in the spaces below to decode the secret message!

PEASHOOTERPEASHOOTERPEASHOOTERPEASHOOTERPEA
SHOOTERSPEASHOOTERPEASHOOTERPEASHOOTERTPEASHOOT
ERPEASHOOTEROPEASHOOTERPEASHOOTERPEASHOOTER
PEASHOOTERPPEASHOOTERPEASHOOTERPEASHOOTEROPEA
SHOOTERPEASHOOTERRPEASHOOTERPEASHOOTERPEASHOOT
ERPEASHOOTERPEASHOOTERPEASHOOTERPEASHOOTERMPEA
SHOOTERPEASHOOTERPEASHOOTERYPEASHOOTERPEASHOOT
ERPEASHOOTERPEASHOOTERPPEASHOOTERPEASHOOTEREPEA
SHOOTERPEASHOOTERPEASHOOTERPEASHOOTERPEASHOOT
ERAPEASHOOTERPEASHOOTERPEASHOOTERWPEASHOOTERPEA
SHOOTERPEASHOOTERIPEASHOOTERPEASHOOTERLPEASHOOT
ERPEASHOOTERPEASHOOTERLPEASHOOTERPEASHOOTERPEA
SHOOTERPEASHOOTERSPEASHOOTERPEASHOOTERHPEASHOOT
ERPEASHOOTEROPEASHOOTERPEASHOOTEROPEASHOOTERPEA
SHOOTERPEASHOOTERTPEASHOOTERPEASHOOTERPEASHOOT
ERPEASHOOTERPEASHOOTERPEASHOOTERPEASHOOTER

STOP OR MAYBE AWLL LBSHO!

Zombie Squares

Two players take turns connecting a line from one zombie head to another. Whoever makes the line that completes the box puts their initials inside the box. The person with the most squares at the end of the game wins!

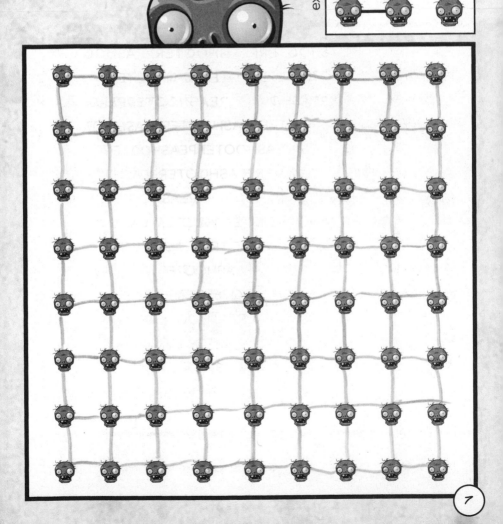

Word Search— For the Love of Zombies

Zombies love to eat one thing and one thing only! Brains! See how many times you can find the word in the puzzle below.

```
D U B P A S Z C J O T S N Z B
Y V E L W T U I B W R Q J B Q
B S W B Q L N Z T R M U Y R C
S R S N X O J P Q Z A A D A K
T P A T L F Z O M B O I S I Y
A G Q I D W O L L R P H N N S
Q H V O N D M U L A P I A S N
F J A K D S B R A I N S A N I
B A L F D S I L V N U M B F A
R Y K M F Y E B Z S A A S L R
A A Q H T I H A R S N I A R B
I P S A S H Y O T A R F Q W L
N E S B F Z K M K X I E C E U
S N U E B X R D A J O N P R V
B R A I N S R E O V F M S T E
```

It's a zombie invasion!
How many zombies
are on this page?

ANSWER

9

9

Secret Code

The zombies are using a secret language. Use the key below to break the code and decipher the secret phrase!

KOZMGH ZIV FTOB ZMW XZM'G WZMXV

pLANTS ARE UGLY CAN_DANCE__.

KEY

A=Z	B=Y	C=X	D=W	E=V	F=U	G=T
H=S	I=R	J=Q	K=P	L=O	M=N	N=M
O=L	P=K	Q=J	R=I	S=H	T=G	U=F
V=E	W=D	X=C	Y=B	Z=A		

Scramblers!

Can you unscramble the letters below to form a real word? Write your answers in the spaces provided.

FLUNERWOS

SUNFLOWER

ROOTESHEPA

PEAShooter

HQUSSA

Squash

What's Different?

Watch out! *This* Pumpkin isn't just for Halloween decoration. Take a good look at the image below, then look at the image on the opposite page.

Can you spot the differences? Write them in the spaces provided.

the Left eye is a moon
the hoot in the nose
it hase howe knok
its liter

Zombie Talk

Zombie and Peashooter have a lot to talk about! Are they arguing? Telling jokes? Sharing recipes? Write their conversation below.

I am going to difet you alld with Mys buls and thar budS and thaa budS.

What's Missing?

Can you pick the piece that solves the puzzle?
Look carefully! Circle the correct piece below.

Draw This!

Can you draw what's inside the box? Let the grid help you draw each section, piece by piece. Take your time and do your best!

Draw here!

Dark Shadows

Can you tell who these zombies are just by their silhouettes? Write your guesses in the spaces below.

Pogo gie

the Leder

Skoba

Make Your Own Zombie

Make up your very own zombie in the space below.
Does he have big red eyes? Is he covered in slime?
Is he happy or sad? Let your imagination run wild!
(And don't forget to give him a name!)

_____

name

Zombie Tales

Uh-oh. It looks like the zombies got hungry and snacked on some words. Read the story below and fill in the blanks so that the story makes sense!

The _Sun_ was shining and the birds were chirping. It was a _beaut_ day for a swim! The family gathered around the _pool_, laying out towels and putting on sunscreen. But as a few tiny _bubbles_ popped up out of the water it was clear that something _sinister_ lurked just beneath the surface. Suddenly and without warning, Snorkel Zombie peeked his head up from the _depths_ and let out a deep cry. "Brains!" he shouted, "_brains_!"

The crowd shrieked in horror, scattering to escape. But Snorkel Zombie wasn't the _fastest_ guy around and by the time he had risen from the pool, there were no more brains around to eat. He _shrugged_ and made his way back into the pool to wait for the next _victim_.

Need some help? Try using these words!

Word Bank

sinister

shrugged

pool

victim

sun

depths

brains

beautiful

fastest

bubbles

Match Game

Each of the plants below uses a special power to protect you from zombie attacks. See if you can figure out which plant uses which projectile and then draw a line to the answer below. Be careful, though, because there are lots of different answers to choose from. Don't get confused!

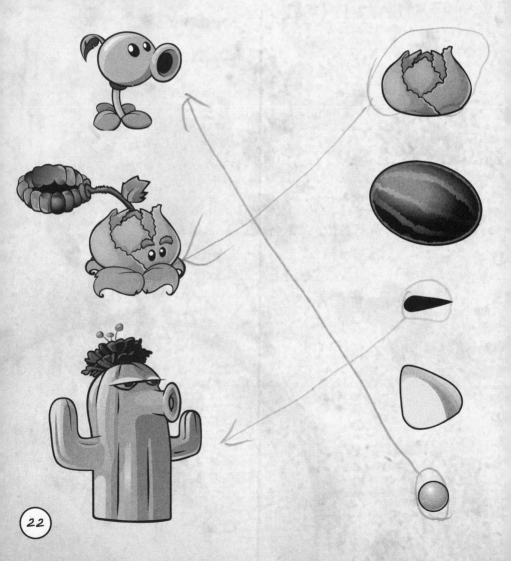

Wonderful Word Maker

What other words can you make from the letters in the word **PEASHOOTER**?

Write your answers in the spaces provided.

Pote

Shoo

Hot

Peas

too

Soot

ape

are

tap

Sap

What's Different?

The monstrous Gargantuar is coming for you!
Take cover! Oh, but before you do that, take a good
look at the image below, then look at the image on
the opposite page.

Can you spot the differences?
Write them in the spaces provided.

he has a bald hed

1 insolator is mising

1 ropis mising

the babes hosterals are misin

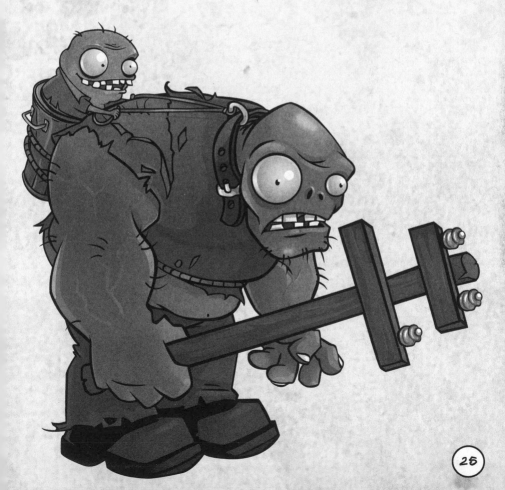

Finish the Picture

Pogo Zombie is really getting a jump on the day.
See if you can finish the drawing below.

Connect the Dots

Who or what is this? Connect the dots to find out!

Create a Story!

It's YOUR turn to come up with a cool story. What will it be about? Maybe you'll write about heroic plants battling evil zombies! Or maybe you'll write about something totally different. It's all up to you! Don't forget to give your story an exciting title.

Title: _____

_____

_____

_____

_____

_____

_____

_____

_____

_____

_____

_____

Maze

Snorkel Zombie is ready for a swim! Help him find his way to the pool in the maze below.

START

FINISH

Tic-Tac-Toe

Two players decide who will be X and who will be O. Player X goes first and makes an X mark in one of the nine sections on the grid below. Then player O takes a turn, marking an O in any empty box. The first player to have three in a row wins!

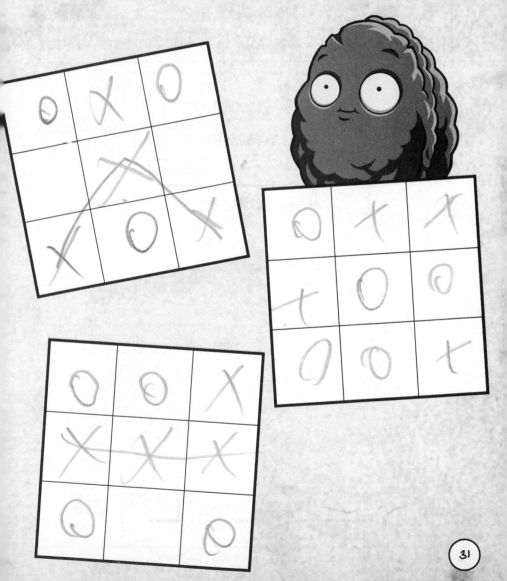

Totally Awesome Trivia

How much do you know about plants? Take a look at the question and see if you can pick the correct answer from the choices below.

The process in which plants get their energy from sunlight is called what?

Sunpower
Steam
Photosynthesis
Awesomeness

Draw a blazing SUN in the
space above and make sure
it looks super cool!

Secret Message

Cross out the name **GIGA GARGANTUAR** every time you see it in the box below. When you spot a letter that doesn't belong, write it in the spaces below to decode the secret message!

```
GIGAGARGANTUARGIGAGARGANTUARGIGAGARGANTUAR
TGIGAGARGANTUARGIGAGARGANTUARHGIGAGARGANTUAR
GIGAGARGANTUARGIGAGARGANTUARAGIGAGARGANTUAR
TGIGAGARGANTUARSGIGAGARGANTUARGIGAGARGANTUAR
GIGAGARGANTUARGIGAGARGANTUAROGIGAGARGANTUAR
GIGAGARGANTUARGIGAGARGANTUARNGIGAGARGANTUAR
GIGAGARGANTUARGIGAGARGANTUARGIGAGARGANTUAR
GIGAGARGANTUAREGIGAGARGANTUARGIGAGARGANTUAR
BGIGAGARGANTUARGIGAGARGANTUARIGIGAGARGANTUAR
GIGAGARGANTUARGIGAGARGANTUARGIGAGARGANTUAR
GIGAGARGANTUARGGIGAGARGANTUARGIGAGARGANTUAR
GIGAGARGANTUARGIGAGARGANTUARGIGAGARGANTUAR
GIGAGARGANTUARZGIGAGARGANTUARGIGAGARGANTUARO
GIGAGARGANTUARGIGAGARGANTUARGIGAGARGANTUARM
GIGAGARGANTUARBGIGAGARGANTUARIGIGAGARGANTUAR
GIGAGARGANTUAREGIGAGARGANTUARGIGAGARGANTUAR
```

THAT'S ONE BIG ZOMBIE.

Yeti Squares

Two players take turns connecting a line from one Zombie Yeti to another. Whoever makes the line that completes the box puts their initials inside the box. The person with the most squares at the end of the game wins!

example

CD

Word Search— Plants-o'-Plenty

Can you spot all these plant names in the puzzle? Keep an eye out for some other plant-related words, too, while you're at it!

T	H	T	O	F	L	N	I	L	F	P	G	E	R	D
E	H	O	H	R	O	U	D	E	K	E	N	L	U	Z
G	X	R	E	G	Q	O	R	M	X	A	I	C	H	G
B	C	T	E	R	I	T	D	A	G	S	L	G	F	N
I	A	L	N	E	I	L	G	T	Z	H	T	B	Q	U
W	S	O	I	L	P	I	N	M	V	O	A	A	Q	A
I	O	W	I	X	G	E	D	U	P	O	G	Q	L	U
D	S	Z	G	J	N	P	A	I	S	T	G	Z	C	W
R	E	T	A	E	P	E	R	T	J	E	S	B	W	D
R	R	Q	Z	J	H	A	C	S	E	R	X	U	C	R
T	A	P	U	L	H	D	F	K	Y	R	U	V	C	N
G	W	V	W	V	H	V	H	O	X	T	G	R	X
Y	K	G	F	I	M	O	X	P	Y	L	Q	L	K	M
S	A	W	U	V	T	R	V	T	H	G	M	Q	Z	L
S	A	A	V	V	U	Q	R	R	N	T	N	R	E	M

FERTILIZER
FOOD
GATLING
PEA
PEASHOOTER

REPEATER
SOIL
SUNLIGHT
THREEPEATER
WATER

Secret Code

The plants are using a secret language. Use the key below to break the code and decipher the secret phrase!

WL MLG UVVW GSV ALNYRVH

DO NOT FEED the ZOMBEIS!

KEY

A=Z	B=Y	C=X	D=W	E=V	F=U	G=T
H=S	I=R	J=Q	K=P	L=O	M=N	N=M
O=L	P=K	Q=J	R=I	S=H	T=G	U=F
V=E	W=D	X=C	Y=B	Z=A		

Scramblers!

Can you unscramble the letters below to form [a] word? Write your answers in the spaces provided.

TRAFSIRTU

_____

MUKNIPP

_____

NEGAMT-OOShRM

_____

Zombie Notes

Zombies love to pass notes back and forth to one another. If only we knew what their notes said! Are they planning a big attack OR a crazy zombie party with all of their friends? Write some notes for them in the spaces provided and make sure to use your best zombie handwriting!

Are these two zombies talking about sports scores?
Who will win the Zombie Games?!

What's Missing?

Can you pick the piece that solves the puzzle?
Look carefully! Circle the correct piece below.

Dark Shadows

Can you tell who these zombies are just by their silhouettes? Write your guesses in the spaces below.

Popo SomBiE

baS ball SOMBiE   cono SomBiE

Draw This!

Can you draw what's inside the box? Let the grid help you draw each section, piece by piece. Take your time and do your best!

Draw here!

Draw This!

Can you draw what's inside the box? Let the grid help you draw each section, piece by piece. Take your time and do your best!

Draw here!

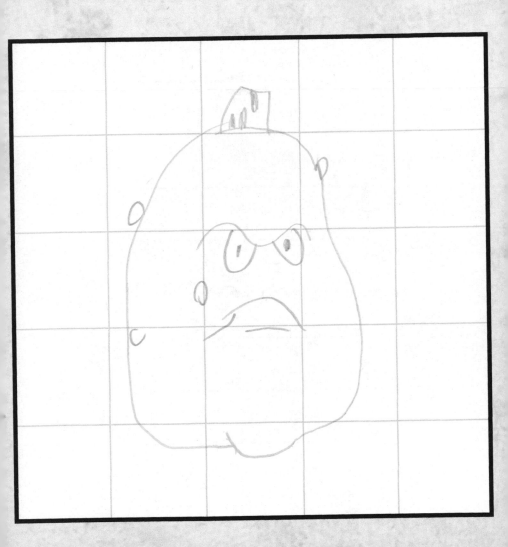

Wonderful Word Maker

What other words can you make from the letters in **POTATO MINE**?

Write your answers in the spaces provided.

_____

_____

_____

_____

_____

_____

_____

_____

_____

Match Game

Each of the plants below uses a special power to protect you from zombie attacks. See if you can figure out which plant uses which projectile, and then draw a line to the answer below. Be careful, though, because there are lots of different answers to choose from. Don't get confused!

Zombie Tales

What lurks in the mysterious cavern? Only YOU know!
Read the story below and fill in the blanks so that the
story makes sense. Or nonsense!

The group of _____ had been hiking in the
mountains for days, searching for a rumored
treasure. No one knew exactly where it was
but an _____ map had led them to a cave, and
the explorers believed this might be the
_____. As they entered the dark cavern, they
could hear a faint_____. Could it be that the
group had disturbed a giant _____?

The _____ shined her flashlight into the
cave to see.

"Brains!!!" cried the Zombie Yeti, awakening
from a deep sleep.

The group had disturbed the beast and
quickly raced to leave the cave. The Zombie
Yeti chased after them and his loud _____
triggered an _____. The explorers made it out
of the cave just in time but the Zombie Yeti
remained trapped behind them in a giant pile
of _____. It was a _____ for another day.

Need some help? Try using these words!

Word Bank

bear

ancient

mystery

snow

growling

explorers

avalanche

footsteps

spot

leader

What's Different?

It's game time with Baseball Zombie. His home runs will have you running for home! Oh, but before you do that, take a good look at the image below, then look at the image on the opposite page.

Can you spot the differences? Write them in the spaces provided.

_____

_____

_____

_____

Finish the Picture

Digger Zombie is on the attack!
See if you can finish the drawing below.

Connect the Dots

Who or *what* is this? Connect the dots to find out!

Create a Story!

Zombies are beating down your door and trying to invade your house! What happens next? Do they teach you how to bake a birthday cake? Are you able to defeat them with just a bag of lemons? How is the Tooth Fairy involved? Create the whole story in the space provided. Don't forget to give your story an exciting title.

Title: _____

_____

_____

_____

_____

_____

_____

_____

_____

_____

_____

_____

_____

_____

_____

_____

_____

_____

_____

_____

_____

_____

_____

_____

_____

Maze

Dancing Zombie is always looking for the next party. But first he needs you to help him get to his backup dancers!

START

FINISH

Tic-Tac-Toe

Two players decide who will be X and who will be O. Player X goes first and makes an X mark in one of the nine sections on the grid below. Then player O takes a turn, marking an O in any empty box. The first player to have three in a row wins!

Totally Fun-Dead Trivia

How much do you know about zombies? Take a look at the question and see if you can pick the correct answer from the choices below.

A zombie's favorite food is what?

Breakfast

Pizza

Brains

Plants

What's your favorite food?
Draw it in the space above!

Secret Message

Cross out the name **SUNFLOWER** every time you see it in the box below. When you spot a letter that doesn't belong, write it in the spaces below to decode the secret message!

SUNFLOWERDSUNFLOWERSUNFLOWERSUNFLOWERSUNFLOWER
SUNFLOWEROSUNFLOWERSUNFLOWERSUNFLOWERSUNFLOWER
SUNFLOWERSUNFLOWERSUNFLOWERNSUNFLOWERSUNFLOWER
SUNFLOWEROSUNFLOWERSUNFLOWERTSUNFLOWERSUNFLOWER
SUNFLOWERSUNFLOWERSUNFLOWERSUNFLOWERSUNFLOWERP
SUNFLOWERSUNFLOWERSUNFLOWERUSUNFLOWERSUNFLOWER
SUNFLOWERTSUNFLOWERSSUNFLOWERSUNFLOWERUSUNFLOW
ERSUNFLOWERNSUNFLOWERSUNFLOWERSSUNFLOWERCSUN
FLOWERSUNFLOWERRSUNFLOWERSUNFLOWERSUNFLOWERESUN
FLOWERSUNFLOWERSUNFLOWERSUNFLOWERESUNFLOWERNSUN
FLOWERSUNFLOWEROSUNFLOWERNSUNFLOWERSUNFLOWER
SUNFLOWERASUNFLOWERSUNFLOWERSUNFLOWERSUNFLOWER
SUNFLOWERSUNFLOWERSUNFLOWERPSUNFLOWEROSUNFLOWER
SUNFLOWERSUNFLOWERTSUNFLOWERASUNFLOWERSUNFLOWER
SUNFLOWERTSUNFLOWEROSUNFLOWERSUNFLOWERSUNFLOWER

_ _   _ _ _   _ _ _   _ _ _ _ _ _ _ _ _
_ _   _   _ _ _ _ _ _ .

Zombie Squares

Two players take turns connecting a line from one Conehead Zombie head to another. Whoever makes the line that completes the box puts their initials inside the box. The person with the most squares at the end of the game wins!

example

CD

63

Word Search— Fog Finder

Can you spot all the words in the puzzle?
Psssst! Here's a secret—they all appear in the Fog Level
of Plants vs. Zombies!

```
N R B L O V E R S W Z P J N P
O Y E F S M B E A A O J A Q T
O N A G R P A T H G N U C V H
L H N S G S L M O J O D K D B
L T V D H I T X A E P W I G R
A X G R A D D M J S A F N O B
B G O A K T Z R A M K S T R H
B O N R E T N A L P U Y H X A
M B M O K C B Y G T X E E Y W
C P C Q F K Q I C G Z T B D P
O F J I H I H A B D C I O E B
D H G G R N C D Y W I Y X B C
G O K Y N W K C R T A W S V P
J J J R L T W J R A E K X L T
K S P L I T P E A X A G B N G
```

SPLIT PEA   CACTUS

DIGGER   PLANTERN

YETI   JACK-IN-THE-BOX

SEA-SHROOM   BLOVER

BALLOON   POGO

Secret Code

The plants are using a secret language. Use the key below to break the code and decipher the secret phrase!

OVG'H SZEV ZM ZDVHLNV KZIGB

_ _ _ ' _ _ _ _ _ _ _

_ _ _ _ _ _ _ _ _ _ _ _ .

KEY

A=Z	B=Y	C=X	D=W	E=V	F=U	G=T
H=S	I=R	J=Q	K=P	L=O	M=N	N=M
O=L	P=K	Q=J	R=I	S=H	T=G	U=F
V=E	W=D	X=C	Y=B	Z=A		

What's Missing?

Can you pick the piece that solves the puzzle?
Look carefully! Circle the correct piece below.

Zombie Notes

What are Buckethead Zombie and Screen Door Zombie saying to each other via their secret notes? Maybe they're writing about the weekend's weather. Buckethead *hates* rain. Write some notes for them in the spaces provided.

These two are up to something.
I can feel it in my bones! I bet *they* can too.

Dark Shadows

Can you tell who these zombies are just by their silhouettes? Write your guesses in the spaces below.

Wonderful Word Maker

What other words can you make from the letters in the word **NEWSPAPER ZOMBIE**?

Write your answers in the spaces provided.

Draw This!

Can you draw what's inside the box? Let the grid help you draw each section, piece by piece. Take your time and do your best!

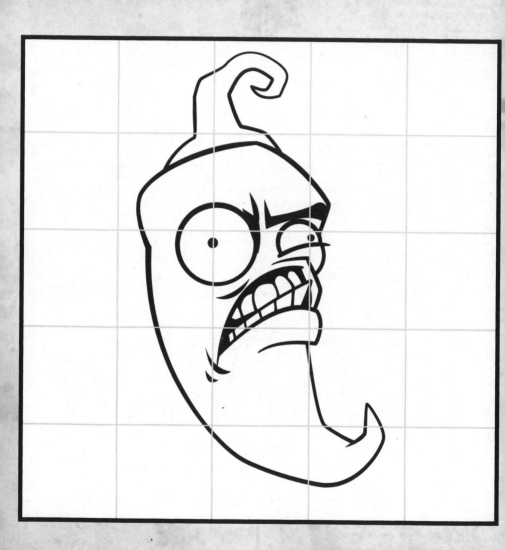

Draw here!

Zombie Tales

Are you ready for a zombie dance off? Read the story below and fill in the blanks so that the story makes sense!

The music was _____ as the couple made their way onto the dance floor. They knew that they'd easily win the competition if they focused on getting their moves right and having fun doing it. As the lights _____, they began their routine. The crowd went_____, loving every minute of it. Then a _____scream stopped everything as Dancing Zombie and his Backup Dancer Zombies arrived on the dance floor. It was time for a dance off! The couple did their _____ as the crowd watched the zombies do some moves of their own. They were popping and _____ up a storm—so much that their zombie _____ fell right off, frightening everyone in attendance. The music ended, and the couple was declared the _____ team! Dancing Zombie and his Backup Dancer Zombies were mad but they _____. You win some, you lose some.

Need some help? Try using these words!

<u>Word Bank</u>

locking

understood

pumping

winning

bloodcurdling

wild

routine

flashed

limbs

What's Different?

What a beautiful day for a dip in the pool. Or is it?! Maybe not with Snorkel Zombie on the prowl. Take a good look at the image below, then look at the image on the opposite page.

Can you spot the differences? Write them in the spaces provided.

Finish the Picture

Cherry Bomb is about to drop!
See if you can finish the drawing below.

Connect the Dots

Who or *what* is this? Connect the dots to find out!

Scramblers!

Can you unscramble the letters below to form a real word? Write your answers in the spaces provided.

MOOGL-HRMOOS

_____

NUS-MSOORH

_____

NERKEL-TUPL

_____

Zombie Pileup!

How many zombies are on this page? Carefully count
how many you see and write your answer in the box.

ANSWER

81

Disgusting Descriptions

Starting with these letters from the alphabet, what words can you use to describe Conehead Zombie?

A_____

B_____

C_____

D_____

E_____

F_____

Match Game

Each of the plants below uses a special projectile to protect itself from zombie attacks. See if you can figure out which plant uses which projectile and then draw a line to the answer below. Be careful, though, because there are lots of different answers to choose from. Don't get confused!

Create a Story!

It's time to come up with a brand-new adventure. What are those zombies up to this time? Create an exciting story in the space provided and don't forget to give your story a cool title.

Title: _____

_____

_____

_____

_____

_____

_____

_____

_____

_____

_____

_____

_____

_____

_____

_____

_____

_____

_____

_____

_____

_____

_____

_____

Maze

Uh-oh. Imp has been separated from Gargantuar! Help him through the maze so he can get back to his friend.

START

FINISH

Tic-Tac-Toe

Two players decide who will be X and who will be O. Player X goes first and makes an X mark in one of the nine sections on the grid below. Then player O takes a turn, marking an O in any empty box. The first player to have three in a row wins!

Totally Awesome Trivia

How much do you know about mushrooms? Take a look at the question and see if you can pick the correct answer from the choices below.

Mushrooms are considered a type of what?

Weed

Flower

Hat

Fungus

Create your own type of funny-looking mushroom in the space above. Give it eyes, ears, and all kinds of crazy stuff!

Secret Message

Cross out the name **SCAREDY-SHROOM** every time you see it in the box below. When you spot a letter that doesn't belong, write it in the spaces below to decode the secret message!

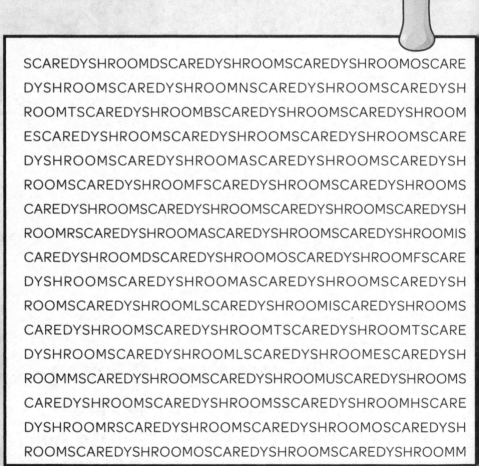

SCAREDYSHROOMDSCAREDYSHROOMSCAREDYSHROOMOSCARE
DYSHROOMSCAREDYSHROOMNSCAREDYSHROOMSCAREDYSH
ROOMTSCAREDYSHROOMBSCAREDYSHROOMSCAREDYSHROOM
ESCAREDYSHROOMSCAREDYSHROOMSCAREDYSHROOMSCARE
DYSHROOMSCAREDYSHROOMASCAREDYSHROOMSCAREDYSH
ROOMSCAREDYSHROOMFSCAREDYSHROOMSCAREDYSHROOMS
CAREDYSHROOMSCAREDYSHROOMSCAREDYSHROOMSCAREDYSH
ROOMRSCAREDYSHROOMASCAREDYSHROOMSCAREDYSHROOMIS
CAREDYSHROOMDSCAREDYSHROOMOSCAREDYSHROOMFSCARE
DYSHROOMSCAREDYSHROOMASCAREDYSHROOMSCAREDYSH
ROOMSCAREDYSHROOMLSCAREDYSHROOMISCAREDYSHROOMS
CAREDYSHROOMSCAREDYSHROOMTSCAREDYSHROOMTSCARE
DYSHROOMSCAREDYSHROOMLSCAREDYSHROOMESCAREDYSH
ROOMMSCAREDYSHROOMSCAREDYSHROOMUSCAREDYSHROOMS
CAREDYSHROOMSCAREDYSHROOMSSCAREDYSHROOMHSCARE
DYSHROOMRSCAREDYSHROOMSCAREDYSHROOMOSCAREDYSH
ROOMSCAREDYSHROOMOSCAREDYSHROOMSCAREDYSHROOMM

_ _ _ ' _ _ _ _ _ _ _ _ _

_ _ _ _ _ _ _ _ _ _ _ _ _ _ _ .

Wall-nut Squares

Two players take turns connecting a line from one Wall-nut to another. Whoever makes the line that completes the box puts their initials inside the box. The person with the most squares at the end of the game wins!

example

CD

Word Search— Up on the Roof

The roof is filled with plants and zombies!
Can you spot them all in the puzzle?

```
C A T P R I F Z R M G F L D D
K A J L G L R E E C A M D G S
G D B B U G R L Q J R B M I S
Y A L B E P O H O S G E M D V
Q L R H A N A L B R A P A Y S
J L L L P G K T X E N S R P H
P Q C U I X E U A H T V R P E
P U L K Z C X P N C U U A O E
J T Z R A B G J U T A S Y F G
T O P R E W O L F L R N F U N
L A D D E R H A Y Z T F P C U
D E U G Q D V O S G O P D L B
T N P T A J I A I C L I Q S T
I C A R Y E M W F F B D K A T
X Y V C O F F E E B E A N B Z
```

BUNGEE

CABBAGE-PULT

CATAPULT

FLOWER POT

MELON-PULT

LADDER

GARGANTUAR

IMP

COFFEE BEAN

GARLIC

Secret Code

The plants are using a secret language. Use the key below to break the code and decipher the secret phrase!

WLM'G VZG YIZRMH

___ ' _ ___ _____.

KEY

A=Z	B=Y	C=X	D=W	E=V	F=U	G=T
H=S	I=R	J=Q	K=P	L=O	M=N	N=M
O=L	P=K	Q=J	R=I	S=H	T=G	U=F
V=E	W=D	X=C	Y=B	Z=A		

Finish the Picture

Threepeater is ready for action!
See if you can finish the drawing below.

Zombie Notes

These zombies might be writing notes about cheeseburgers OR world domination. We just don't know! Write the zombie notes in the spaces provided.

Hmmmm. I wonder if they like ketchup.

Dark Shadows

Can you tell who these zombies are just by their silhouettes? Write your guesses in the spaces below.

Wonderful Word Maker

What other words can you make from the letters in **UMBRELLA LEAF**?

Write your answers in the spaces provided.

Draw This!

Can you draw what's inside the box? Let the grid help you draw each section, piece by piece. Take your time and do your best!

Draw here!

Zombie Tales

It's game day for Football Zombie! Read the story below and fill in the blanks so that the story makes sense!

It was the day of the big game, and everyone was _____! The coach of the football team called all his players into the _____ to give them a pep talk.

"Go out there tonight and _____ to win!" he said. "Be _____ and dont be afraid of anything!"

Without _____, Football Zombie burst into the locker room, letting out a deep _____ at the assembled _____.

"Run for your life!" the _____ shouted.

The _____ scattered and screamed as they ran away in fear. Football Zombie stood there for a moment, confused.

"Well, so much for not being afraid of _____!" The coach laughed.

Need some help? Try using these words!

Word Bank

players

team

fight

snarl

anything

excited

quarterback

locker room

warning

strong

What's Different?

Jack-in-the-Box Zombie has a little surprise for you. Be careful! Take a good look at the image below, then look at the image on the opposite page.

Can you spot the differences? Write them in the spaces provided.

Connect the Dots

Who or *what* is this? Connect the dots to find out!

Scramblers!

Can you unscramble the letters below to form a real word? Write your answers in the spaces provided.

KIPKSOCRE

_____

DARMLOGI

_____

LOMEN-TPUL

_____

Make Your Own Plant

Design your very own plant in the space below.
Is it big and green? Does it have lots of leaves?
Is it tiny or gigantic? Let your imagination run wild!
(And don't forget to give it a name!)

name

Zombie Pileup!

How many zombies are on this page? Carefully count how many you see and write your answer in the box.

ANSWER

Disgusting Descriptions

What words can you use to describe Zombie Yeti using these letters from the alphabet?

G _____

H _____

I _____

J _____

K _____

L _____

M _____

Secret Message

Cross out the name **SPIKEWEED** every time you see it in the box below. When you spot a letter that doesn't belong, write it in the spaces below to decode the secret message!

```
SPIKEWEEDASPIKEWEEDSPIKEWEEDLSPIKEWEEDSPIKEWEEDSPIKE
WEEDWSPIKEWEEDSPIKEWEEDASPIKEWEEDSPIKEWEEDSPIKE
WEEDSPIKEWEEDYSPIKEWEEDSPIKEWEEDSSPIKEWEEDSPIKE
WEEDSPIKEWEEDSPIKEWEEDSPIKEWEEDSPIKEWEEDSPIKEWEED
SPIKEWEEDSPIKEWEEDSPIKEWEEDSPIKEWEEDSPIKEWEEDSPIKE
WEEDSPIKEWEEDSPIKEWEEDSPIKEWEEDWSPIKEWEEDSPIKE
WEEDSPIKEWEEDSPIKEWEEDESPIKEWEEDSPIKEWEEDESPIKE
WEEDDSPIKEWEEDSPIKEWEEDSPIKEWEEDSPIKEWEEDOSPIKE
WEEDUSPIKEWEEDTSPIKEWEEDSPIKEWEEDSPIKEWEEDSPIKE
WEEDSPIKEWEEDSPIKEWEEDSPIKEWEEDSPIKEWEEDSPIKE
WEEDTSPIKEWEEDSPIKEWEEDSPIKEWEEDSPIKEWEEDSPIKE
WEEDHSPIKEWEEDSPIKEWEEDESPIKEWEEDSPIKEWEEDPSPIKE
WEEDSPIKEWEEDRSPIKEWEEDOSPIKEWEEDSPIKEWEEDBSPIKE
WEEDSPIKEWEEDSPIKEWEEDSPIKEWEEDLSPIKEWEEDSPIKEWEED
SPIKEWEEDESPIKEWEEDSPIKEWEEDSPIKEWEEDSPIKEWEEDM
SPIKEWEEDSPIKEWEEDSPIKEWEEDSPIKEWEEDSPIKEWEED
```

_ _ _ _ _ _   _ _ _ _   _ _ _

_ _ _   _ _ _ _ _ _ _ _.

Create a Story!

It's dinnertime and the zombies are hungry for brains! But where do zombies go to eat dinner? Do they get into a food fight? Do they use napkins? It's your turn to tell the rest of the story in the space provided.

Title:_____

_____

_____

_____

_____

_____

_____

_____

_____

_____

_____

_____

_____

_____

_____

_____

_____

_____

_____

_____

_____

_____

_____

_____

Maze

Pole-Vaulting Zombie is getting a little jumpy. Help him release his nervous energy by leading him through the maze below.

START

FINISH

Tic-Tac-Toe

Two players decide who will be X and who will be O. Player X goes first and makes an X mark in one of the nine sections on the grid below. Then player O takes a turn, marking an O in any empty box. The first player to have three in a row wins!

Word Search—
Pool Party

There's a pool party and all the plants and zombies
are invited! Find them all in the puzzle.

```
D Y P N A B B X E E H R R Y O
U I Q Q T O B A V H M E S N E
K X V H B R Y R P D T F X G B
K B M S T I F Q Z A N D J W U
D K L B F A Q J E M C D D T T
N E J W M U H P A I S R C X Y
D T A N G L E K E L P H B Y K
F W S A E E C Y H Y A R T V C
B X C G R T U B O S H P X H U
I X D H P A A Q P K A E E R D
K K T R L L J R G G O U O N Q
M J B Z L L E K R O N S Q L O
R N Z N H N K O H T X T H S O
K S E S R U T L W P Z F R B C
L I J W W T I R J W R T V W F
```

DUCKY TUBE

SQUASH

BOBSLED

JALAPEÑO

THREEPEATER

TANGLEKELP

TALL-NUT

SNORKEL

Secret Code

The plants are using a secret language. Use the key below to break the code and decipher the secret phrase!

WLM'G OVG ALNYRVH
GFIM BLF RMGL HZOZW

_ _ _ ' _ _ _ _ _ _ _ _ _ _

_ _ _ _ _ _ _ _ _ _ _ _ _ _ _.

KEY

A=Z	B=Y	C=X	D=W	E=V	F=U	G=T
H=S	I=R	J=Q	K=P	L=O	M=N	N=M
O=L	P=K	Q=J	R=I	S=H	T=G	U=F
V=E	W=D	X=C	Y=B	Z=A		

Zombie Notes

These zombies are up to something sinister. Or are they? If only we knew what they were writing notes about. That's where you come in. Write some notes for them in the spaces provided.

Dark Shadows

Can you tell who these zombies are just by their silhouettes? Write your guesses in the spaces below.

_____

_____

_____

Wonderful Word Maker

What other words can you make from the letters in **BUCKETHEAD ZOMBIE**?

Write your answers in the spaces provided.

Draw This!

Can you draw what's inside the box? Let the grid help you draw each section, piece by piece. Take your time and do your best!

Draw here!

Zombie Tales

Billy is about to have a zombie birthday he'll never forget. Read the story below and fill in the blanks so that the story makes sense!

"Happy Birthday, Billy!" the boy's mother shouted as he entered the room. It was Billy's big day, and all of his friends _____ him with a big _____. The house was filled with _____ and a table of presents sat in the corner. There was a knock at the door. Perhaps one of the _____ was late to the party. Billy _____ opened it to find Balloon Zombie floating there _____.

"Brains?" the zombie asked.

Billy _____ the door shut and began _____ as his friends ran in all different _____. Balloon Zombie looked up at the number on the door and realized he was at the wrong house.

"Oooops," he thought, as he slowly made his way to the next-door neighbors' _____ for lunch.

Need some help? Try using these words!

<u>Word Bank</u>

screaming

party

directions

house

surprised

cheerfully

slobbering

guests

slammed

balloons

Scramblers!

Can you unscramble the letters below to form a real word? Write your answers in the spaces provided.

EEEWDIKPS

_____

ÑALPEAJO

_____

DOWROCHOT

_____

Secret Message

Cross out the name **UMBRELLA LEAF** every time you see it in the box below. When you spot a letter that doesn't belong, write it in the spaces below to decode the secret message!

UMBRELLALEAFUMBRELLALEAFUMBRELLALEAFUMBRELLALEA
FUMBRELLALEAFLUMBRELLALEAFUMBRELLALEAFEUMBRELLA
LEAFUMBRELLALEAFUMBRELLALEAFAUMBRELLALEAFUMBREL
LALEAFUMBRELLALEAFFUMBRELLALEAFUMBRELLALEAFUMBREL
LALEAFUMBRELLALEAFUMBRELLALEAFUMBRELLALEAFUMBREL
LALEAFUMBRELLALEAFUMBRELLALEAFMUMBRELLALEAFUMBREL
LALEAFUMBRELLALEAFUMBRELLALEAFEUMBRELLALEAFAUMBREL
LALEAFUMBRELLALEAFUMBRELLALEAFUMBRELLALEAFUMBREL
LALEAFUMBRELLALEAFUMBRELLALEAFUMBRELLALEAFUMBRELLA
LEAFLUMBRELLALEAFOUMBRELLALEAFUMBRELLALEAFUMBREL
LALEAFUMBRELLALEAFUMBRELLALEAFUMBRELLALEAFUMBREL
LALEAFNUMBRELLALEAFUMBRELLALEAFUMBRELLALEAFUMBREL
LALEAFEUMBRELLALEAFUMBRELLALEAFUMBRELLALEAF

_ _ _ _   _ _   _ _ _ _ _.

Word Search— Day Break

It's a beautiful day outside (unless you're a zombie)! See if you can find the plants that appear during the day in the puzzle.

F	N	F	D	L	R	E	Y	D	K	W	U	A	R	M
R	E	T	O	O	H	S	A	E	P	A	X	X	E	A
B	O	V	E	K	B	S	N	L	Z	T	N	X	W	K
Y	M	O	J	P	W	I	L	B	R	E	E	Y	O	N
V	T	O	K	T	H	K	I	Y	E	R	U	S	L	L
X	E	X	B	S	R	X	R	G	N	P	Z	P	F	L
W	D	Z	N	Y	A	E	Q	R	E	J	O	F	N	J
C	N	U	B	X	R	Q	E	W	P	T	V	B	U	G
Z	S	S	V	B	H	R	N	S	A	I	A	E	S	V
W	A	L	L	N	U	T	E	T	Z	I	S	M	U	P
Z	O	Y	D	O	Q	U	O	H	V	A	X	K	B	P
U	I	P	E	M	Z	M	W	Z	C	Q	B	H	X	P
J	D	M	R	S	I	J	D	U	I	X	M	D	J	A
Z	K	M	B	N	V	C	B	M	B	A	M	Y	C	G
K	T	C	E	A	U	R	F	G	U	V	J	Z	B	X

SUNFLOWER   WALL-NUT

POTATO MINE   PEASHOOTER

TREES   CHERRY BOMB

SUNSHINE   WATER

Secret Code

The plants are using a secret language. Use the key below to break the code and decipher the secret phrase!

WLM'G VZG BLFI EVTVGZYOVH,
GSVB SZEV UVVORMTH

_ _ _ ' _   _ _ _   _ _ _ _   _ _ _ _ _ _ _ _ _ _ ,

_ _ _ _   _ _ _ _   _ _ _ _ _ _ _ _ .

KEY

A=Z	B=Y	C=X	D=W	E=V	F=U	G=T
H=S	I=R	J=Q	K=P	L=O	M=N	N=M
O=L	P=K	Q=J	R=I	S=H	T=G	U=F
V=E	W=D	X=C	Y=B	Z=A		

Wonderful Word Maker

What other words can you make from the letters
in **WINTER MELON**?

Write your answers in the spaces provided.

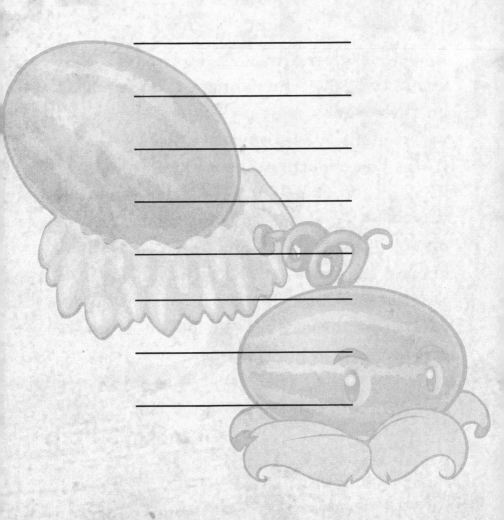

_____

_____

_____

_____

_____

_____

_____

Zombie Tales

It's a day at the races for Pole-Vaulting Zombie. Or is it?! Read the story below and fill in the blanks so that the story makes sense!

A hush fell over the _____ as the race was about to begin. The runners stood anxiously on their marks, waiting for the signal.

"Brains!!!" a deep voice grumbled from _____. It was Pole-Vaulting Zombie and he was_____ ! The _____ took off in different _____ while screaming for help. But this zombie had his eye on a different _____ and slowly made his way around the track, much to the _____ of the assembled crowd. This was a race, not a pole vault. The zombie suddenly looked _____ and stopped dead in his tracks.

"Wrong place," the zombie thought, dropping his _____ and walking off into the _____.

Need some help? Try using these words!

<u>Word Bank</u>

runners

prize

confused

pole

directions

woods

beyond

crowd

hungry

surprise

133

Scramblers!

Can you unscramble the letters below to form a real word? Write your answers in the spaces provided.

MIBOZE

_____

MOCHEPR

_____

EATPEERR

_____

Secret Message

Cross out the name **PLANTERN** every time you see it in the box below. When you spot a letter that doesn't belong, write it in the spaces below to decode the secret message!

PLANTERNLPLANTERNPLANTERNPLANTERNPLANTERNPLANTERN
PLANTERNPLANTERNPLANTERNPLANTERNIPLANTERNPLANTERN
PLANTERNPLANTERNGPLANTERNHPLANTERNTPLANTERNPLANT
ERNPLANTERNPLANTERNPLANTERNPLANTERNUPLANTERNPLANT
ERNPLANTERNPLANTERNPLANTERNPLANTERNPPLANTERNPLANT
ERNPLANTERNPLANTERNTPLANTERNPLANTERNPLANTERNPLANT
ERNHPLANTERNPLANTERNPLANTERNEPLANTERNPLANTERNPLAN
TERNPLANTERNPLANTERNPLANTERNPLANTERNPLANTERNPLAN
TERNZPLANTERNPLANTERNPLANTERNOPLANTERNPLANTERN
PLANTERNPLANTERNMPLANTERNPLANTERNPLANTERNBPLANT
ERNPLANTERNPLANTERNPLANTERNIPLANTERNPLANTERNPLANT
ERNPLANTERNPLANTERNPLANTERNPLANTERNPLANTERNPLANT
ERNPLANTERNEPLANTERNPLANTERNPLANTERNPLANTERNPLANT
ERNPLANTERNPLANTERNPLANTERNPLANTERNPLANTERNPLANT
ERNPLANTERNPLANTERNSPLANTERNPLANTERNPLANTERNPLANT
ERNPLANTERNPLANTERNPLANTERNPLANTERNPLANTERN

_ _ _ _ _ _ _ _ _ _ _ _ _ _ _ _ _.

Dark Shadows

Can you tell who these zombies are just by their silhouettes? Write your guesses in the spaces below.

Sunflower Squares

Two players take turns connecting a line from one Sunflower to another. Whoever makes the line that completes the box puts their initials inside the box. The person with the most squares at the end of the game wins!

example

CD

Word Search—Nightmare!

Night has fallen and strange happenings are afoot! See if you can find all the plants and zombies in the puzzle.

```
B K G I G A F O O T B A L L C
A E Q N E N N I H P P P M B V
C B A C H K I V A X F V F K W
K M N S K P T C U K C C S U Q
U A M M U F D M N Z D K S G N
P Q O X O N M J F A O J J J E
D M O G D O S K P B D D H R W
A D R Q C F R H J P G R A J S
N X H H C G Z H R P S F C O P
C P S M O O R H S O N P Y H A
E D E G X M M N D F O U M A P
R E M L L A B T O O F M G F E
K P U Z K W H Z M T R U A X R
F N F Y Y X H M H D T V P N Y
G R A V E B U S T E R F L F H
```

NEWSPAPER

PUFF-SHROOM

FUME-SHROOM

HYPNO-SHROOM

FOOTBALL

BACKUP DANCER

DANCING

GIGA-FOOTBALL

SUN-SHROOM

GRAVE BUSTER

Secret Code

The plants are using a secret language. Use the key below to break the code and decipher the secret phrase!

YV XZIVUFO. KOZMGH DZMG
GL HKVMW ZOO BLFI NLMVB.

__ _____. _____ ____

__ _____ ___ ____ _____.

KEY

A=Z	B=Y	C=X	D=W	E=V	F=U	G=T
H=S	I=R	J=Q	K=P	L=O	M=N	N=M
O=L	P=K	Q=J	R=I	S=H	T=G	U=F
V=E	W=D	X=C	Y=B	Z=A		

Wonderful Word Maker

What other words can you make from the letters in the word **SUNFLOWER**?

Write your answers in the spaces provided.

_____

_____

_____

_____

_____

_____

_____

Zombie Tales

What's the top story in Newspaper Zombie's world? Read the story below and fill in the blanks so that the story makes sense!

It was a _____ day at the park and the flowers smelled as _____ as can be. Mary and Ken delicately laid out their picnic blanket for an _____ lunch on the grass. But something smelled very bad and neither of them knew where it was coming from. They spotted what _____ to be a man on a nearby _____ bench who was _____ a newspaper, and they decided to ask him if he knew what was causing the _____. As they got closer they realized that it wasn't a man on the _____, it was Newspaper Zombie! The couple grabbed their things, _____ for help, and ran away in fright. Newspaper Zombie let out a big yawn and continued reading his _____.

Need some help? Try using these words!

Word Bank

park

bench

stench

gorgeous

screamed

sweet

newspaper

enjoyable

appeared

reading

Scramblers!

Can you unscramble the letters below to form a real word? Write your answers in the spaces provided.

CDYAERS-OOMRHS

_____

CEI-HOROSM

_____

OMOD-ORMHOS

_____

Secret Message

Cross out the name **GRAVE BUSTER** every time you see it in the box below. When you spot a letter that doesn't belong, write it in the spaces below to decode the secret message!

```
GRAVEBUSTERNGRAVEBUSTERGRAVEBUSTERGRAVEBUSTER
GRAVEBUSTEROGRAVEBUSTERGRAVEBUSTERGRAVEBUSTER
GRAVEBUSTERGRAVEBUSTERGRAVEBUSTERGRAVEBUSTERZ
GRAVEBUSTEROGRAVEBUSTERGRAVEBUSTERGRAVEBUSTER
MGRAVEBUSTERGRAVEBUSTERGRAVEBUSTERBGRAVEBUSTER
GRAVEBUSTERIGRAVEBUSTEREGRAVEBUSTERSGRAVEBUSTER
GRAVEBUSTERGRAVEBUSTERGRAVEBUSTERGRAVEBUSTER
GRAVEBUSTERAGRAVEBUSTERGRAVEBUSTERGRAVEBUSTER
GRAVEBUSTERLGRAVEBUSTERGRAVEBUSTERGRAVEBUSTER
GRAVEBUSTERGRAVEBUSTERGRAVEBUSTERGRAVEBUSTER
GRAVEBUSTERGRAVEBUSTERGRAVEBUSTERGRAVEBUSTER
GRAVEBUSTERLGRAVEBUSTEROGRAVEBUSTERGRAVEBUSTER
WGRAVEBUSTERGRAVEBUSTERGRAVEBUSTERGRAVEBUSTER
EGRAVEBUSTERGRAVEBUSTERGRAVEBUSTERGRAVEBUSTER
GRAVEBUSTERGRAVEBUSTERGRAVEBUSTERDGRAVEBUSTER
GRAVEBUSTERGRAVEBUSTERGRAVEBUSTERGRAVEBUSTER
```

__ _____ _____.

Party Time

Could it be that plants and zombies have called a truce? Is the war over? In the spaces provided, write some dialogue for the plants and zombies to tell their story.

Are they whispering about a secret?
I wonder if it's about parties.

Dark Shadows

Can you tell who these zombies are just by their silhouettes? Write your guesses in the spaces below.

_____

_____

_____

What's Missing?

Can you pick the piece that solves the puzzle?
Look carefully! Circle the correct piece below.

Draw This!

Can you draw what's inside the box? Let the grid help you draw each section, piece by piece. Take your time and do your best!

Draw here!

What's Different?

Step carefully or you'll get pulled underwater by Tangle Kelp's slimy tendrils. Take a good look at the image below, then look at the image on the opposite page.

Can you spot the differences? Write them in the spaces provided.

_____

_____

_____

_____

Maze

Football Zombie can't find his way to the game. Help him get through the maze below so he won't miss it!

START

FINISH

Tic-Tac-Toe

Two players decide who will be X and who will be O. Player X goes first and makes an X mark in one of the nine sections on the grid below. Then player O takes a turn, marking an O in any empty box. The first player to have three in a row wins!

Zombie Notes

Evil is afoot! It looks like Zombot and Dr. Zomboss might be planning a vacation. Where could they be going? Write a few notes for them in the spaces provided.

Word Search– Daymare

Zombies love to come out and play during the daytime. Take a look at the puzzle and try finding the names of all the zombies that enjoy basking in the sunlight!

```
G N I T L U A V E L O P N I X
D D N G V O C I J Y B A J V B
M A D U Q K O G L X C K R J P
R B E U A C Q D F H C E E E I
O Z M H N N C Z S N Y X M X R
O F O K T Z Q A T J P I U P A
D W W M P E R W A L L N U T M
N B O P B T K G U V A V X A D
E I P Y H I D C L R I O Y R D
E M T L S V E S U R S S L G O
R C T E D G X B V B K X W E B
C Y Z F Y C N S F B M T T T Y
S O D T O A H W S K P V O V U
B N G B A V E W X H P N V F Y
M A M S L I F A I X J I L J O
```

ZOMBIE   BUCKETHEAD

TARGET   WALL-NUT

TRASH CAN   SCREEN DOOR

POLE-VAULTING

Secret Code

The plants are using a secret language. Use the key below to break the code and decipher the secret phrase!

YV MRXV GL KOZMGH

__ ____ __ _____.

KEY

A=Z	B=Y	C=X	D=W	E=V	F=U	G=T
H=S	I=R	J=Q	K=P	L=O	M=N	N=M
O=L	P=K	Q=J	R=I	S=H	T=G	U=F
V=E	W=D	X=C	Y=B	Z=A		

Wonderful Word Maker

What other words can you make from the letters in the word **TORCHWOOD**?

Write your answers in the spaces provided.

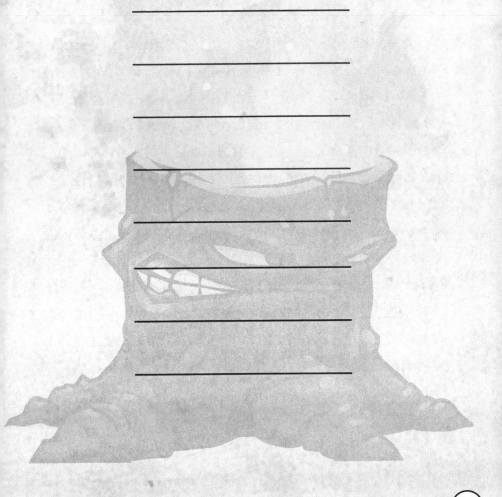

_____

_____

_____

_____

_____

_____

_____

_____

Zombie Tales

Zombies get into trouble everywhere. Even on the high seas! Read the story below and fill in the blanks so that the story makes sense!

"Daddy, look!" the little _____ shouted from the boat. "I think I see a fishy!"

The boy's father had taken him on a boat ride, and they were having so much fun trying to spot _____ kinds of fish in the water. Something about this one looked _____, and as it got closer the _____ spotted what appeared to be an old man in the _____. But this was neither man nor _____. He was Dolphin Rider Zombie and he was headed straight for the _____! Zombies are quite slow and the boat quickly _____ away, leaving the zombie _____ and his dolphin _____treading water by themselves.

Need some help? Try using these words!

<u>Word Bank</u>

different

zoomed

boat

water

ghoul

boy

different

friend

fish

father

Scramblers!

Can you unscramble the letters below to form a real word? Write your answers in the spaces provided.

HDAOENEC

_____

PRSEAWNEP

_____

ALLT-UTN

_____

Secret Message

Cross out the name **MARIGOLD** every time you see it in the box below. When you spot a letter that doesn't belong, write it in the spaces below to decode the secret message!

MARIGOLDAMARIGOLDMARIGOLDMARIGOLDMARIGOLDMARI
GOLDMARIGOLDLMARIGOLDLMARIGOLDMARIGOLDMARIGOLD
MARIGOLDTMARIGOLDHMARIGOLDMARIGOLDMARIGOLDMARI
GOLDMARIGOLDMARIGOLDAMARIGOLDMARIGOLDTMARIGOLD
MARIGOLDMARIGOLDGMARIGOLDMARIGOLDLMARIGOLDIMARI
GOLDTMARIGOLDMARIGOLDMARIGOLDTMARIGOLDMARIGOLD
MARIGOLDEMARIGOLDRMARIGOLDMARIGOLDMARIGOLDMARI
GOLDMARIGOLDMARIGOLDSMARIGOLDIMARIGOLDMARIGOLD
MARIGOLDMARIGOLDMARIGOLDMARIGOLDMARIGOLDSMARIGOLD
MARIGOLDMARIGOLDMMARIGOLDMARIGOLDMARIGOLDAMARI
GOLDRMARIGOLDIMARIGOLDMARIGOLDMARIGOLDMARIGOLD
MARIGOLDMARIGOLDMARIGOLDMARIGOLDMARIGOLDMARIGOLD
MARIGOLDMARIGOLDMARIGOLDGMARIGOLDMARIGOLDOMARI
GOLDMARIGOLDMARIGOLDMARIGOLDLMARIGOLDDMARIGOLD
MARIGOLDMARIGOLDMARIGOLDMARIGOLDMARIGOLD

___ ____ _____ __
_____.

165

Draw This!

Can you draw what's inside the box? Let the grid help you draw each section, piece by piece. Take your time and do your best!

Draw here!

Wonderful Word Maker

What other words can you make from the letters in the word **STARFRUIT**?

Write your answers in the spaces provided.

_____

_____

_____

_____

_____

_____

_____

_____

_____

Pea Squares

Two players take turns connecting a line from one Peashooter to another. Whoever makes the line that completes the box puts their initials inside the box. The person with the most squares at the end of the game wins!

example

CD

What's Different?

Don't call Torchwood a fiery stump or you're bound to feel the heat! Take a good look at the image below, and then look at the image on the opposite page.

Can you spot the differences? Write them in the spaces provided.

_____

_____

_____

_____

Maze

Dr. Zomboss is up to something sinister. But first he needs your help to find his way through this winding maze!

START

FINISH

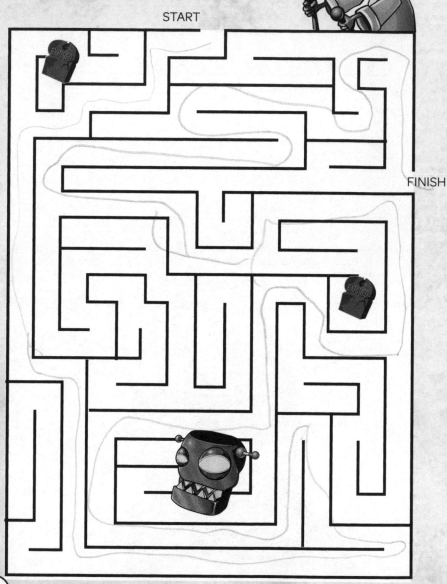

What's Missing?

Can you pick the piece that solves the puzzle?
Look carefully! Circle the correct piece below.

Zombie Notes

Gargantuar and Imp are best pals! Do you think they go to a lot of fun parties together? Maybe they're going to one tonight, and they're giving each other crazy directions for how to get there! Write a few notes for them in the spaces provided.

Design a Zombie

Design your very own zombie in the space below. Does he have a wild hairstyle? Does he have ten arms? Let your imagination run wild! (And don't forget to give him a name!)

_____

name

Scramblers!

Can you unscramble the letters below to form a real word? Write your answers in the spaces provided.

PIM

_____

RD. BOZOMSS

_____

MOBTOZ

_____

177

Zombie Tales

A good zombie is always ready to rock and roll. Read the story below and fill in the blanks so that the story makes sense!

The _____ was about to begin, and the roar of the crowd was very _____. Everyone was excited to see their favorite band play. The stage went black and music began to play. It was time to rock out! Multicolored _____ lit up the arena as the crowd went _____.

Suddenly a loud scream cut through the _____ as Buckethead Zombie _____ out from behind the curtain and onto the _____. The band stopped playing. They were _____ by the sight.

"Brains!!!" shouted Buckethead Zombie as he picked up a _____ and started playing. The band looked at one another and smiled. Rock and roll will never die, even when it's _____!

Need some help? Try using these words!

Word Bank

sound

laser lights

guitar

frightened

stumbled

undead

concert

loud

stage

wild

Dark Shadows

Can you tell who these zombies are just by their silhouettes? Write your guesses in the spaces below.

_____

_____

_____

Secret Message

Cross out the name **HYPNO-SHROOM** every time you see it in the box below. When you spot a letter that doesn't belong, write it in the spaces below to decode the secret message!

```
HYPNOSHROOMYHYPNOSHROOMHYPNOSHROOMOHYPNOSH
ROOMHYPNOSHROOMUHYPNOSHROOMAHYPNOSHROOMRHYP
NOSHROOMHYPNOSHROOMHYPNOSHROOMEHYPNOSHROOM
HYPNOSHROOMHYPNOSHROOMHYPNOSHROOMHYPNOSHROOM
HYPNOSHROOMGHYPNOSHROOMHYPNOSHROOMEHYPNOSH
ROOMHYPNOSHROOMTHYPNOSHROOMHYPNOSHROOMTHYP
NOSHROOMIHYPNOSHROOMHYPNOSHROOMHYPNOSHROOM
HYPNOSHROOMNHYPNOSHROOMHYPNOSHROOMGHYPNOSH
ROOMHYPNOSHROOMHYPNOSHROOMVHYPNOSHROOMEHYP
NOSHROOMRHYPNOSHROOMHYPNOSHROOMYHYPNOSHROOM
HYPNOSHROOMHYPNOSHROOMHYPNOSHROOMHYPNOSHROOM
HYPNOSHROOMSHYPNOSHROOMHYPNOSHROOMLHYPNOSH
ROOMHYPNOSHROOMEHYPNOSHROOMHYPNOSHROOMEHYP
NOSHROOMHYPNOSHROOMHYPNOSHROOMPHYPNOSHROOM
HYPNOSHROOMHYPNOSHROOMYHYPNOSHROOMHYPNOSH
ROOMHYPNOSHROOMHYPNOSHROOMHYPNOSHROOM
```

_ _ _   _ _ _   _ _ _ _ _ _ _

_ _ _ _   _ _ _ _ _ _ ...

Connect the Dots

Who or what is this? Connect the dots to find out!

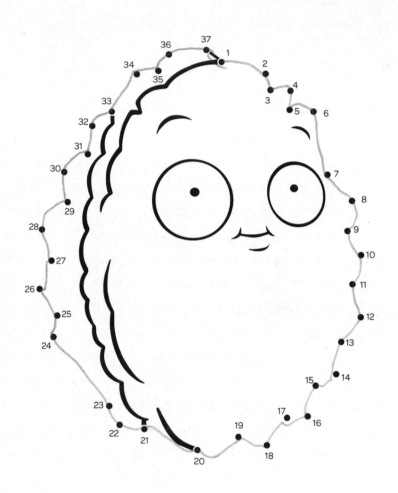

Flower Power

How many Sunflowers are on this page?
Carefully count how many you see and write your
answer in the box below.

ANSWER

11

Delightful Descriptions

What words can you use to describe Marigold starting with these letters from the alphabet?

N

P

R

S

T

W

What's Missing?

Can you pick the piece that solves the puzzle?
Look carefully! Circle the correct piece below.

Totally Awesome Trivia

How much do you know about zombies? Take a look at the question and see if you can pick the correct answer from the choices below.

Zombies actually prefer eating Brain Pies over Brain Cookies

    A) True

    B) False

    C) All of the above

What face would you make if you saw a big, scary zombie coming for you? Draw a picture of your expression in the space above!

Secret Code

The plants are using a secret language.
Use the key below to break the code and decipher
the secret phrase!

DZGVI BLFI KOZMGH

_ _ _ _ _   _ _ _ _   _ _ _ _ _ _.

KEY

A=Z	B=Y	C=X	D=W	E=V	F=U	G=T
H=S	I=R	J=Q	K=P	L=O	M=N	N=M
O=L	P=K	Q=J	R=I	S=H	T=G	U=F
V=E	W=D	X=C	Y=B	Z=A		

Wonderful Word Maker

What other words can you make from the letters in the word **SPIKEWEED**?

Write your answers in the spaces provided.

_____

_____

_____

_____

_____

_____

_____

_____

_____

Word Search— Zombies Rule!

All right, so we know zombies love brains—but what other words pop into your head when you think of the fun-dead? See if you can find some in the puzzle.

```
H C Y L D C A A H H S I D J G
P S T E D M Z F X Q C G A W S
K C I F I Y Y O A M W S E T O
S Q O L L R Y L N L P F D K R
D W K U Y C Z N A O H T N G B
V K O N R T Q D O Q C V U C I
L H L A I N S K I S G W F G E
G S Z H S T E H U N G R Y T R
L Y P G H R A X V B N E R R J
R F I O R F I D Z X E C H W Y
D G C I R J V K Y E N M H X U
N A F Q Y T C F J W H E E K K
B I C A N X Y Y M H L S F K P
C I T S A T P E E R C S J B J
R R S Q K F E H G E B Y S F F
```

GHOULY CRAZY
CREEPTASTIC SPORTY
STYLISH FUN-DEAD
HUNGRY SPOOKERRIFIC
MESSY

Zombie Tales

What's that hiding in the toy store? Could it be Pogo Zombie? Read the story below and fill in the blanks so that the story makes sense!

It had been a long day at the _____, and Mr. Johnson was ready to close down and head home for some _____. As he counted the money from the _____, he heard a _____ noise coming from behind one of his _____.

"Who is that? Who's back there?" he shouted, hoping it was just a _____. He quickly grabbed a _____ and began making his way back toward the display to check things out. As he _____ the corner, he was shocked to find Pogo Zombie there _____ up and down on his pogo stick. Mr. Johnson _____ in fear and ran out of the store, leaving the poor zombie by himself.

Need some help? Try using these words!

Word Bank

mouse

jumping

yelped

displays

dinner

cash register

toy store

rustling

rounded

broom

Secret Message

Cross out the name **STARFRUIT** every time you see it in the box below. When you spot a letter that doesn't belong, write it in the spaces below to decode the secret message!

STARFRUITSTARFRUITSTARFRUITRSTARFRUITSTARFRUITSTAR
FRUITSTARFRUITESTARFRUITASTARFRUITSTARFRUITSTARFRUIT
STARFRUITSTARFRUITCSTARFRUITSTARFRUITHSTARFRUITSTAR
FRUITSTARFRUITSTARFRUITSTARFRUITSTARFRUITSTARFRUITSTAR
FRUITSTARFRUITFSTARFRUITSTARFRUITSTARFRUITSTARFRUITSTAR
FRUITOSTARFRUITSTARFRUITRSTARFRUITSTARFRUITSTARFRUITT
STARFRUITSTARFRUITSTARFRUITHSTARFRUITSTARFRUITSTAR
FRUITSTARFRUITSTARFRUITSTARFRUITSTARFRUITSTARFRUITSTAR
FRUITESTARFRUITSTARFRUITSTARFRUITSTARFRUITSTARFRUIT
STARFRUITSTARFRUITSTARFRUITSTARFRUITSSTARFRUITSTARFRUIT
STARFRUITSTARFRUITSTARFRUITTSTARFRUITSTARFRUITSTAR
FRUITSTARFRUITSTARFRUITSTARFRUITSTARFRUITSTARFRUITSTAR
FRUITSTARFRUITASTARFRUITSTARFRUITSTARFRUITRSTARFRUIT
STARFRUITSTARFRUITSSTARFRUITSTARFRUITSTARFRUITSTAR
FRUITSTARFRUITSTARFRUITSTARFRUITSTARFRUITSTARFRUIT

_ _ _ _ _   _ _ _   _ _ _   _ _ _ _ _!

Make Your Own Plant

Design your very own plant in the space below. Is it
big and green? Does it have lots of leaves? Is it tiny or
gigantic? Let your imagination run wild!
(And don't forget to give it a name!)

_____

name

What's Different?

The spikes of a Cactus can be pretty prickly. Take a good look at the image below, then look at the image on the opposite page.

Can you spot the differences? Write them in the spaces provided.

Draw This!

Can you draw what's inside the box? Let the grid help you draw each section, piece by piece. Take your time and do your best!

Draw here!

Dark Shadows

Can you tell who these zombies are just by their silhouettes? Write your guesses in the spaces provided.

_____

Scramblers!

Can you unscramble the letters below to form a real word? Write your answers in the spaces provided.

LTFOBOLA

_____

GANCDIN

_____

KLNESOR

_____

What's Missing?

Can you pick the piece that solves the puzzle?
Look carefully! Circle the correct piece below.

Maze

Jalapeño Zombie is looking hot! If only he wasn't trapped in zombie jail! Help him find a way out using the maze below.

START

FINISH

Tic-Tac-Toe

Two players decide who will be X and who will be O.
Player X goes first and makes an X mark in one of the
nine sections on the grid below. Then player O takes a
turn, marking an O in any empty box. The first
player to have three in a row wins!

Design a Zombie

Design your very own zombie in the space below. Does he have big red eyes? Is he covered in slime? Is he happy or sad? Let your imagination run wild! (And don't forget to give him a name!)

_____

name

What's Missing?

Can you pick the piece that solves the puzzle?
Look carefully! Circle the correct piece below.

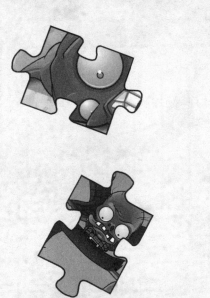

Maze

Zombie Yeti is lost! Help him yodel his way back home in the maze below.

START

FINISH

Tic-Tac-Toe

Two players decide who will be X and who will be O. Player X goes first and makes an X mark in one of the nine sections on the grid below. Then player O takes a turn, marking an O in any empty box. The first player to have three in a row wins!

Zombie Reviews

These zombies are yapping about a movie they just saw! What are they saying? Did they love it? Will they see it again? Or was it a big stinker? Write their notes in the spaces provided.

Draw This!

Can you draw what's inside the box? Let the grid help you draw each section, piece by piece. Take your time and do your best!

Draw here!

What's Different?

What's a Plantern? Why, it's a plant lantern, of course!
Take a good look at the image below, then look at the
image on the opposite page.

Can you spot the differences?
Write them in the spaces provided.

_____

_____

_____

_____

Answer Key

Page 4:
Sunlight

Page 6:
Stop or my pea will shoot!

Page 8:

Page 9:
9 zombies

Page 10:
Plants are ugly
and can't dance.

Page 11:
Sunflower
Peashooter
Squash

Pages 12–13:

Page 15:

Page 18:
Pole-Vaulting
Flag
Snorkel

Page 22:

Pages 24–25:

Page 27:

Page 30:

Page 32:
Photosynthesis

Page 34:
That's one big zombie.

Page 37:

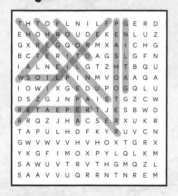

Page 38:
Do not feed the zombies.

Page 39:
Starfruit
Pumpkin
Magnet-shroom

Page 42:

Page 43:
Baseball
Pogo
Conehead

Page 49:

Pages 52–53:

Page 55:

Page 58:

Page 60:
Brains

Page 62:
Do not put sunscreen on a potato.

Page 65:

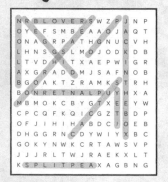

Page 66:
Let's have an awesome party!

Page 67:

Page 70:
Newspaper
Jack-in-the-Box
Football

Pages 76–77:

Page 79:

Page 80:
Gloom-shroom
Sun-shroom
Kernel-pult

Page 81:
13 zombies

Page 83:

Page 86:

Page 88:
Fungus

Page 90:
Don't be afraid of a little mushroom.

Page 93:

Page 94:
Don't eat brains.

Page 98:
Buckethead
Dolphin Rider
Gargantuar

Pages 104-105:

Page 106:

Page 107:
Spikerock
Marigold
Melon-pult

Page 109:
11 zombies

Page 111:

Always weed out the problem.

Page 114:

FINISH

Page 117:

Page 118:

Don't let zombies turn you into salad.

Page 120:

Screen Door
Zombie Yeti
Imp

Page 126:

Spikeweed
Jalapeño
Torchwood

Page 127:

Leaf me alone.

Page 129:

Page 130:

Don't eat your vegetables they have feelings.

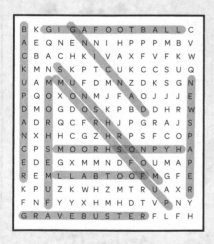

Page 154:

Page 165:

All that glitters is Marigold.

Pages 170-171:

Page 159:

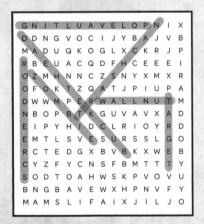

Page 172:

Page 160:

Be nice to plants.

Page 164:

Conehead
Newspaper
Tall-Nut

Page 173:

Page 177:
Imp
Dr. Zomboss
Zombot

Page 180:
Bungee
Digger
Ducky Tube

Page 181:
You are getting very sleepy . . .

Page 182:

Page 183:
11 Sunflowers

Page 185:

Page 186:
They love anything
with brains. (Answer: C)

Page 188:
Water your plants.

Page 191:

Page 194:
Reach for the stars!

Pages 196-197:

Pages 200–201:
Bobsled Team
Buckethead
Prospector

Page 202:
Football
Dancing
Snorkel

Page 203:

Page 204:

Page 207:

Page 208:

Pages 214–215: